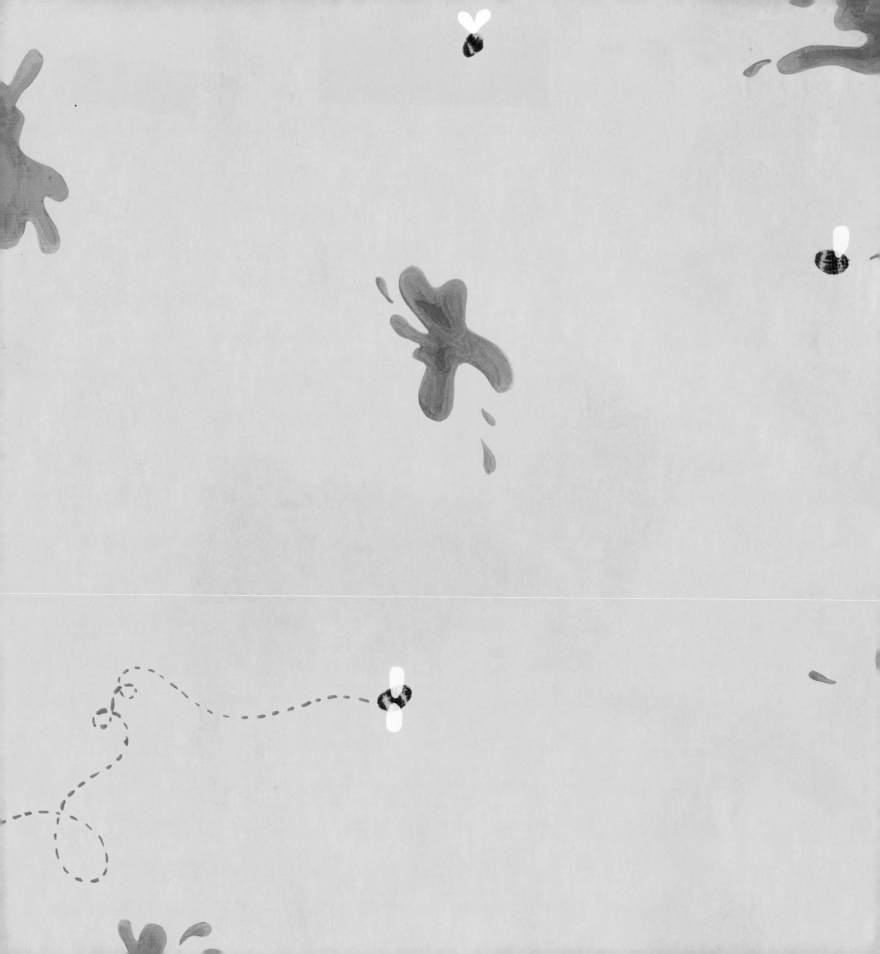

To Joe, Tim, Tom, Susie, Nancy, Kay, Karla, and Bob. Being the baby
of this crew is the best! You should be jealous.

-jg

Little ✦ BOOST is published by
Picture Window Books
A Capstone Imprint
1710 Roe Crest Drive
North Mankato, Minnesota 56003
www.capstonepub.com

Library of Congress Cataloging-in-Publication data is
available on the Library of Congress website.

ISBN 978-1-4048-6797-0 (library binding)

Printed in the United States of America in North Mankato, Minnesota.
102011   006405CGS12

Lucille
Gets
Jealous

written by Julie Gassman

illustrated by Charlotte Cook

PICTURE WINDOW BOOKS

a capstone imprint

Lucille was **jealous**
of her friends at school.

She was **jealous**
of the boy across the street.

And Lucille was especially jealous of her little sister,
Margaret.

Every day, something happened to make Lucille
a bit more jealous of Margaret.

One day, Margaret drew all over the kitchen table with markers. Did she get in **trouble**?

No! But Lucille did, for leaving the markers out.

Another time, Lucille was all set to watch **Fashion Fairies.**

"Lucille, I need to make supper, and Margaret is a little whiney,"
Mom said. "Please let her watch Cuddle Cats."

by Julie Gassman
crabby
pants

Illustrated by Richard Watson

When lucille's grandma came to visit, everything Margaret did impressed her.

"Oh, my honey bear can say 'book'!" Grandma exclaimed.

"Big deal," whispered lucille. "I can actually read!"

"Oh, my honey bear can fetch her shoes!" Grandma said.

"It's not like she puts them on **herself**," mumbled Lucille.

"Oh, my honey bear can eat with a spoon!"
Grandma cheered.

"That's not even hard!" muttered Lucille.

Grandma was even impressed with how Margaret slept.

"Oh, that Margaret is the sweetest little honey bear!" Grandma whispered to Mom.

"Why doesn't anybody see that
I'm **sweet,** too?" wondered Lucille.

And just like that,
Lucille knew what
she needed to do.

She walked straight
into the kitchen
and went to work.

When Grandma made her way into the kitchen, she found quite the surprise.

"Lucille! What are you doing?" she asked.

"I'm becoming a **honey bear** like Margaret," Lucille said. "Then you will think I am **sweet** and **smart** and **funny**, too!"

"Oh, Lucille," said Grandma. "You don't need to cover yourself with honey. I already know you are all those things. And you are a **wonderful** big sister on top of it all."

"I am?" asked Lucille.

"You are," said Grandma. "That is why Margaret is growing into such a nice little girl. She's watching you!"

Lucille thought about all the times she played with Margaret.

"Oh," said Lucille. "I guess you're right."

"Now lets clean up this mess before your mom sees. This can be our secret, my lovely little ladybug," Grandma said.

Lucille's smile shined right through the honey.
She didn't feel jealous of Margaret anymore.

In fact, she didn't feel jealous of **anyone**.

She did, however, feel quite sticky.